Fat Cat

for Gavin – J.S.

for Dr J.S.G. Simmons – R.A.

First published in hardback in Great Britain by HarperCollins*Publishers* Ltd in 2002
First published in paperback by Collins Picture Books in 2003

1 3 5 7 9 10 8 6 4 2

ISBN: 0-00-664726-X

Collins Picture Books is an imprint of the Children's Division, part of HarperCollins*Publishers* Ltd.

The HarperCollins website address is: www.**fire**and**water**.com

Printed and bound in China

Fat Cat

James Sage
illustrated by Russell Ayto

An imprint of HarperCollinsPublishers

Farmer Big lived next door to Farmer Bluster...

who lived next door to Farmer Smarts... and
they each thought their cornfield was the best.

"No doubt about it!" boasted Farmer Big, "my cornfield is the best!"

"It isn't!" argued Farmer Bluster, "my cornfield is much better than yours."

Now Farmer Smarts knew that his cornfield was really better than either of his neighbours', but he was much too modest to say so.

One day, much to the dismay of all three farmers, they discovered that mice had been eating the young corn.

"Jumping Jehosophat!"
groaned Farmer Big.

"Would you believe it!"
moaned Farmer Bluster.

"Dear, oh dear!" mumbled
Farmer Smarts.

To teach those mice a lesson they would never forget, Farmer Big and Farmer Bluster each set to work building the perfect mousetrap.

And they hammered and twisted and pushed and pounded away all day and most of the night and part of the next day, too.

"By Jingo, those mice will soon learn who's boss around here!" bragged Farmer Big.

"With my invention they don't stand a chance!" gloated Farmer Bluster.

And when they had finished they just couldn't help sneaking over to inspect the other's mousetrap.

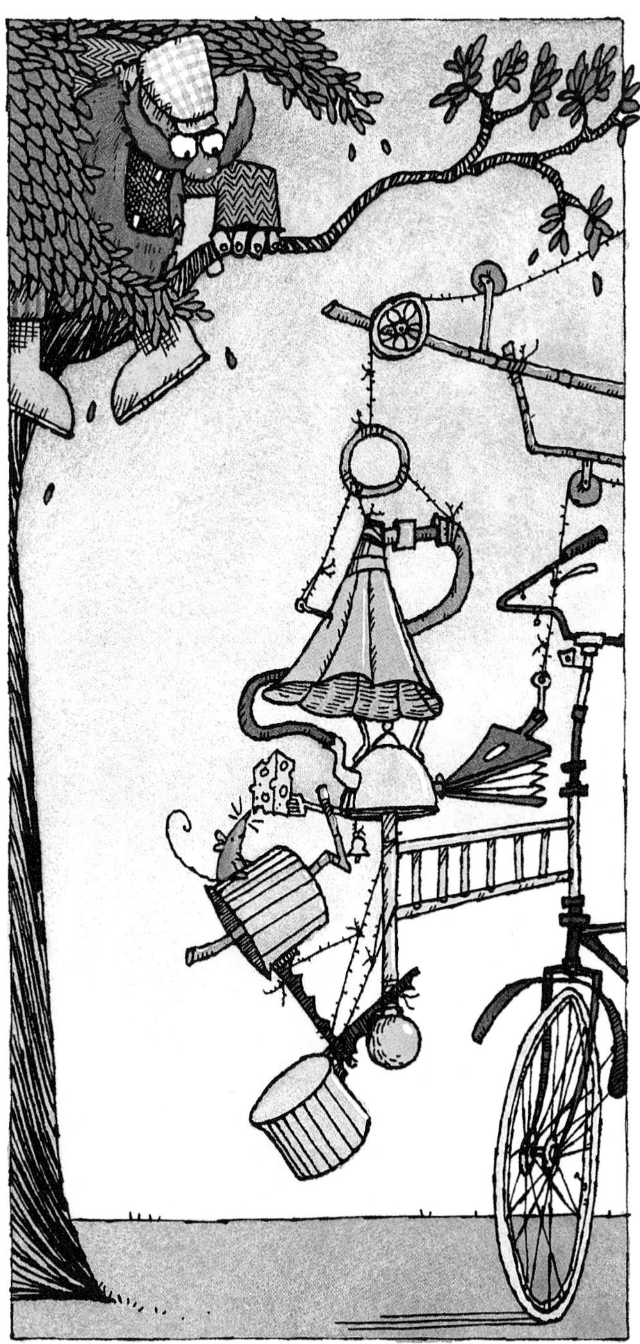

"A non-starter if ever I saw one!" smirked Farmer Big.

"He hasn't the foggiest!" snickered Farmer Bluster.

But there was a teensy-weensy problem that neither had considered. It seemed the mice weren't interested in either mousetrap.

They had better things to think about.

While the mice stuffed themselves, the cornfield of Farmer Smarts remained strangely untouched.

Which is what they did.

And it wasn't long before they discovered the real reason behind Farmer Smarts' brilliant success at getting rid of the mice.

WHAT A
Get out while the going's good!

FAT
CAT!
Phooey!
A cat with
attitude!
Cripes!
Time to
fade!
Goodbye-eee!
Toodle-oo!

And Farmer Big looked at Farmer Bluster, and Farmer Bluster looked at Farmer Big, and they decided there and then to pinch Farmer Smarts' highly efficient mouse catcher.

They left no stone unturned, yet Fat Cat was nowhere to be seen.

"Can't win for losing, it seems," muttered Farmer Big.
"You can say that again, old Buddy!" sighed
Farmer Bluster.

"Now, now, my friends, there's no need to feel glum," said Farmer Smarts. "I think what you may be looking for is over there... resting in the hay. Only she's not quite so fat any more."

And sure enough, there was Fat Cat, slimmer and prettier and very, very pleased with herself.
"KITTENS!" exclaimed Farmer Big.
"A WHOLE LITTER!" gasped Farmer Bluster.

"Now you too can have a foolproof mouse catcher," beamed Farmer Smarts.

And once the kittens had grown into fat cats themselves, the fields of Farmer Big and Farmer Bluster were soon looking every bit as good as that of Farmer Smarts.

But secretly all three farmers still thought their cornfield was the best!

Every child deserves the best...

0-00-664627-1

0-00-715002-4

0-00-710794-3

0-00-713728-1

0-00-664775-8

0-00-710624-6

0-00-664777-4

0-00-712735-9

0-00-714011-8

0-00-664646-8

Collins Picture Books